This book belongs to:

Thanks to Janet Jenvey and also to the staff of the London Library for their help with research —A.D.

The Cosmic Professor :
The Story of Albert Einstein

超級科學家系列
SUPER SCIENTISTS

宇宙教授：

愛因斯坦的故事

Andrew Donkin 著

Gillian Hunt 繪

錢怡君 譯

三民書局

The bright boys, they all study maths,
And Albert Einstein points the paths,
Although he seldom takes the air,
We wish to God he'd cut his hair.

普林斯頓的學生

$E=MC^2$

The janitor

Princeton, USA —1949

I would probably
never have met Albert
Einstein at all if Spider
hadn't tried so hard to
spoil our baseball game.

We were all playing
in the street using my
brand-new ball. Spider
was **jealous** and I knew
he'd try and **ruin** things
if he could.

門房

美國普林斯頓，*1949年*

　　如果不是史派特那麼費盡心思地要破壞我們的棒球賽，我可能一輩子也不會遇見亞伯・愛因斯坦。

　　當時我們正在街上打棒球，用的是我那顆全新的球，而史派特是個善妒的人，所以我很清楚，他不會錯過任何一個搗蛋的機會。

janitor [`dʒænətɚ] 名 門房，
　房屋的管理人
spoil [spɔɪl] 動 破壞
brand-new [`bræn`nju] 形
　嶄新的，全新的
jealous [`dʒɛləs] 形 善妒嫉的
ruin [`ruɪn] 動 毀壞

⑤

I didn't have to wait long. The first chance he got, he gave the ball a **massive** hit, **deliberately** sending it **spinning** over the houses **opposite**.

The other kids turned and ran. We were always getting into trouble for breaking windows wherever we played.

The ball sailed clean over the houses. Spider gave me an evil look as I **set off** to find it.

First, I had to climb over the fence at the back of the houses. I jumped up to get a **grip** and just about made it over. The ball wasn't there, though, and I had to **sneak** through a hole in the fence to next door.

沒有很久，他的第一次機會就來了。他奮力一擊，故意讓球旋轉飛向對面的房子。

其他的孩童全轉身跑了。我們每在一個地方玩球，總會因為打破窗戶而惹上麻煩。

球乾淨俐落地飛越過那些房子。當我準備去尋找那顆球時，史派特不懷好意地看了我一眼。

首先，我得要翻過那些房子後面的圍籬，我往上一躍，緊緊地撐住，剛好翻過。然而球不在那裡，於是我必須鑽過籬笆上的一處小洞到隔壁人家去找。

massive [`mæsɪv] 形 大而重的
deliberately [dɪ`lɪbərɪtlɪ] 副 故意地
spin [spɪn] 動 旋轉
opposite [`ɑpəzɪt] 形 對面的
set off 動身，出發
grip [grɪp] 名 緊緊的抓住
sneak [snik] 動 偷偷行動

I looked through the window at the back of the house. Inside, the walls of the rooms were covered with books. Nothing but books.

I started kicking away leaves, looking for my ball. I must have made more noise than I meant to because the next thing I knew, the back door creaked open.

我從屋後的窗子朝裡面看了看。房間裡頭的四面牆上全都是書，除了書以外還是書。

我踢開樹葉找球。我絕對是弄出了太大的聲音，因為接下來，後門嘎吱一聲開了。

"**C**an I help?" called a voice.

An old man with **untidy** white
hair came slowly down the
porch steps.

He wore a **loose** gray sweater that was all
pulled **out of shape** and a pair of **baggy**
trousers. He looked like a janitor or maybe the
gardener.

「需要我幫忙嗎?」一個聲音說。

一位頭髮凌亂的白髮老先生緩慢步下門廊的階梯。

他穿著一件拉扯得全走了樣的寬鬆灰毛衣,以及一件鬆垮垮的褲子。他看起來像個門房,也有可能是個園丁。

untidy [ʌn`taɪdɪ] 形 凌亂的

porch [portʃ] 名 門廊

loose [lus] 形 寬鬆的

out of shape 走樣,變形

baggy [`bægɪ] 形 (褲子等)寬鬆下垂的

"**W**hat is it that you've lost?" he said walking toward me.

I should probably have run for it, but I told him about Spider and the ball.

"What was its **trajectory**?" he asked.

"What?"

"Where did it come from?" he said **patiently**.

I pointed to where we'd been playing. He held out his hand along the same **angle**.

"I've looked and it's not here," I said. "It must have landed someplace else."

The old man reached up, **grabbed** the lowest branch of the tree and shook it. The ball fell down and landed by his feet.

13

「你掉了什麼東西？」他邊走向我邊問。

或許我那時應該要掉頭跑掉的，但是我沒有，我還告訴他史派特和那顆球的事。

「你知道球飛行的軌道嗎？」他問。

「什麼？」

「球是從哪兒來的呢？」他耐心地說。

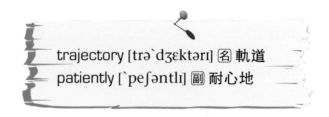

trajectory [trəˋdʒɛktərɪ] 图 軌道
patiently [ˋpeʃəntlɪ] 副 耐心地

我指著我們剛才玩球的地方。他順著我指的地方伸出了手。

　　「我已經找過了，但是球不在這兒。」我說。「它一定是掉在別處了。」

　　老先生將手往上一伸，握住這棵樹最低的枝幹搖了搖。球掉了下來，就掉在他的腳邊。

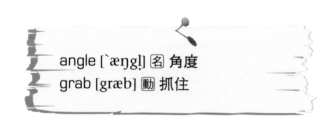

angle [ˋæŋgḷ] 名 角度
grab [græb] 動 抓住

"There," smiled the old man. "Not many people get to **rescue** a baseball from Professor Einstein's back yard."

So this was Albert Einstein's house. Even I had heard of him. He was a big time scientist.

"Do you work for him?"

"We work on the same things," said the old man, showing me through the house toward the front door. "Do you know much about Professor Einstein's work?"

He talked to me like I was a person rather than just a kid.

「在這兒，」老先生微微一笑。「會來愛因斯坦教授的後院救回棒球的人並不多。」

　　原來，這就是亞伯‧愛因斯坦的家。連我都聽說過他，他可是當代了不起的大科學家呢！

rescue [ˋrɛskju] 勔 拯救

「你替他工作嗎？」

「我們從事相同的研究工作，」老先生邊說，邊帶著我穿過房子走向前門。「你知道很多有關愛因斯坦教授研究工作的事嗎？」

他對我說話的態度，彷彿我是個大人，而不只是個小孩子而已。

"**H**e discovered the **universe or something**, didn't he?" I said. The old man frowned.

There was a small pile of books on a table in the hall. I saw Einstein's name on the top one and picked it up.

ALBERT EIN

"Here, he does **stuff** no one can understand — like this." I started to **flick** through the book. It was all **mathematics** and pages of really long words.

「他發現了宇宙那方面的事，不是嗎？」我說。老先生皺了皺眉。

在大廳的桌上有一小堆書，我看見最上面一本有著愛因斯坦的名字，便拿起了那本書。

「你瞧，他盡做些沒人能懂的玩意兒——就像這個。」我逐頁翻了起來，全都是數學以及一頁頁又臭又長的字句。

universe [`junə,vɝs] 名 宇宙
...or something …之類的，諸如此類的
stuff [stʌf] 名 物，東西
flick [flɪk] 動 輕拂
mathematics [,mæθə`mætɪks] 名 數學

Then, at the front of the book, I found a picture. It was a photo of the old man. Underneath the picture were printed the words 'Albert Einstein'.

He gave a **sheepish** smile and showed me out.

Outside, I threw the ball high into the air and caught it with a satisfying **thud**.

Einstein. I had met Einstein.

接著，在書的扉頁，我發現有張照片，正是這位老先生的照片，照片下方印著——「亞伯・愛因斯坦」。

他不好意思地對我笑了笑，然後帶著我走出屋外。

到了外面，我把球高高地丟到空中，心滿意足地砰一聲接住。

愛因斯坦，我遇見了愛因斯坦！

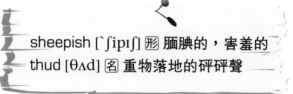

sheepish [`ʃipɪʃ] 形 腼腆的，害羞的
thud [θʌd] 名 重物落地的砰砰聲

The smartest man in the world

The first thing I did afterwards was get a book out of the library. It was called *Einstein and* **Relativity**.

It said Einstein had been born in Germany and was **Jewish**. When **the Nazis** (Adolf Hitler and that lot) **took over** in the thirties he had to **flee** to another country. He chose America.

世上最聰明的人

　　之後我所做的第一件事就是去圖書館借了本書，書名是
《愛因斯坦與相對論》。

　　書上說，愛因斯坦在德國出生，是個猶太人。當納粹（希
特勒一類的人）在1930年代接掌大權後，他必須逃到其他國
家。於是他選擇了美國。

relativity [,rɛlə`tɪvətɪ] 名 相對論
Jewish [`dʒuɪʃ] 形 猶太人的
the Nazis [`nɑtsɪz] 名 納粹黨
　　（1919年在德國成立的國
　　家社會主義德意志勞工黨，
　　以Adolf Hitler為首）
take over　接管
flee [fli] 動 逃

Einstein didn't **invent** things or build machines, he **came up with** ideas. **Pure** ideas about the way that the universe worked.

His **theories** were all about space, time, and the speed of light. Einstein was now the most famous scientist in the entire world.

愛因斯坦並沒有發明東西或是建造任何機器,他有的只是種種的想法,有關宇宙運作方式的純理論概念。

　　他的理論全繞著空間、時間以及光速打轉。愛因斯坦現在是全世界最有名的科學家。

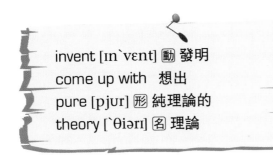

invent [ɪnˋvɛnt] 動 發明
come up with　想出
pure [pjʊr] 形 純理論的
theory [ˋθiərɪ] 名 理論

Dad told me a story about how a man was driving through Princeton when he saw Einstein walking down the street. The man was so surprised that he drove his car into a tree!

I had a Show and Tell coming up next month. (Show and Tell is this terrible thing where you have to stand in front of the class and talk for ten minutes. I really hate them.) I had to pick a science subject and Einstein was perfect.

　　爸爸說了一個故事給我聽，說有一名男子開車經過普林斯頓時，因為看見了走在街上的愛因斯坦，那名萬分驚訝的男子結果連人帶車一頭撞上了樹！

　　下個月就輪到我「秀秀說說」了。（「秀秀說說」是件極恐怖的事，你必須站在全班同學面前講十分鐘的話。這是我最討厭的活動了。）我必須選一個科學方面的主題，而愛因斯坦可說是最佳的題材。

I read the book, but I didn't understand that much. I was **desperate** to talk to him again. I was even thinking of **organizing** another baseball game, just so old Spider could **whack** the ball into his back yard again. But I needn't have worried.

我是讀完了那本書，不過我並不是十分瞭解。我迫切地想要再和他談談，甚至還想過要再辦一次棒球賽，如此一來，史派特這老兄才能再一次使勁地把球打到他家後院，只不過這一次我一點也不擔心。

desperate [ˋdɛspərɪt] 形 極想要的
organize [ˋɔrgənˌaɪz] 動 組織
whack [hwæk] 動 猛擊

About a week later, I was on my way home from school and I saw Einstein standing on a street corner. He looked a little lost.

"Ah, the baseball boy," said Einstein, smiling as he saw me coming.

Einstein **leaned** down and **whispered** into my ear. "I've been walking and thinking about my work and...well, I seem to have forgotten where my house is."

大約一個禮拜後，在我放學回家的路上，我看見愛因斯坦就站在街角，看起來有些茫然。

　　「啊！棒球小子。」愛因斯坦看到我走來時微笑著說。

　　愛因斯坦斜過身來，湊在我耳邊小聲地說：「我一直邊走邊想著我的研究，然後……嗯！我好像就忘了我家在哪裡了。」

lean [lin] 動 傾身
whisper [`hwɪspɚ] 動 低聲說

He was a bit **embarrassed**. I'd heard that he was always doing things like this when he **was wrapped up in** his science.

"**No sweat**, I can get you home."

As we walked across town, Einstein saw me looking down at his feet. He was wearing house **slippers** and had no socks on.

"**I** have to **devote** my time to **physics** so I need to reduce everything else to a **minimum**. That is why I do not waste time at barbers' shops," he said brushing back his long white hair.

他有點兒不好意思。我曾聽說，每當他埋首於科學研究時，總會發生類似的事情。

「小事一樁，我可以帶你回家。」

當我們走過市中心時，愛因斯坦看到我低頭瞧著他的腳，他腳上穿的是室內拖鞋而且沒穿襪子。

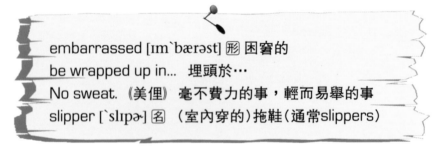

embarrassed [ɪm`bærəst] 形 困窘的
be wrapped up in... 埋頭於…
No sweat. 《美俚》 毫不費力的事，輕而易舉的事
slipper [`slɪpɚ] 名 （室內穿的）拖鞋（通常slippers）

「我得把全部的時間投注在物理上，所以我必須把其他的雜事減到最少，這就是為什麼我不要把時間浪費在理髮店的緣故。」他邊說邊將他那頭長長的白髮往後撥。

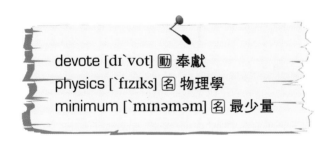

devote [dɪ`vot] 動 奉獻
physics [`fɪzɪks] 名 物理學
minimum [`mɪnəməm] 名 最少量

On Main Street we came to the 'Baltimore', everyone's favorite ice-cream **parlor**.

"When I arrived in America, the very first thing I did was to go in here and have an ice-cream cone," said Einstein. "Come on, I'll buy you one for showing me home."

He ordered two cones all right, but he didn't have any money. Not a **dime**. His pockets **were stuffed with calculations** and **formulas**, but no money.

我們來到緬因街上的「巴爾的摩」，那是大家最喜歡的冰淇淋店。

　　「剛到美國時，我所做的第一件事，就是來這裡買一份冰淇淋甜筒。」愛因斯坦說。「來吧！我請你一客，就算謝謝你帶我回家。」

　　於是他馬上點了二客，但是他卻沒有帶錢，一毛也沒有。他的口袋裡塞滿了算式及公式，就是沒有錢。

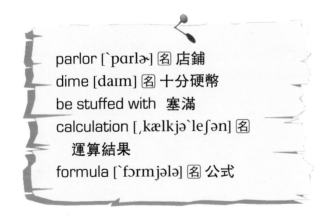

parlor [`pɑrlɚ] 名 店鋪
dime [daɪm] 名 十分硬幣
be stuffed with　塞滿
calculation [ˌkælkjə`leʃən] 名
　　運算結果
formula [`fɔrmjələ] 名 公式

This was my chance.

"I'll tell you what," I said. "You **explain** to me how the universe works, and *I'll* buy the ice-cream!"

The smartest man in the world took a big lick of his strawberry cone and **grinned**.

"Done," he said.

我的機會來了。

　　「我看這樣好了，」我說，「你解釋宇宙的運作方式給我聽，那冰淇淋就算我的！」

　　這個世界上最聰明的人舔了一大口草莓冰淇淋，滿足地咧開嘴笑了。

　　「成交。」他說。

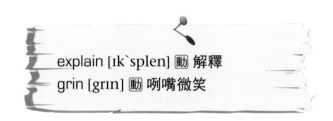

explain [ɪk`splen] 動 解釋
grin [grɪn] 動 咧嘴微笑

Einstein's cosmos

Einstein loved sailing. He was good at it too. Next day, we went out to Carnegie Lake where he kept his boat.

"I like sailing because I am lazy," he said as we climbed onboard, "and this is the sport that **demands** the least **energy**."

愛因斯坦的宇宙

　　愛因斯坦熱愛駕船航行，也是箇中好手。第二天，我們前往卡內基湖，也就是他停放船隻的地方。

　　「我喜歡航行，因為我很懶，」當我們登上船時，他這麼說，「這是最不耗費力氣的運動。」

cosmos [`kɑzməs] 名 宇宙
demand [dɪ`mænd] 動 需要
energy [`ɛnɚdʒɪ] 名 精力

We set off toward the center of the lake.

"Relativity is easy," he said, jumping straight into the subject.

Einstein didn't waste time. He tried never to waste time.

"When you sit with a pretty girl for two hours, it seems like only a minute. Yes? But when you are having your teeth **drilled** in a **dentist**'s chair, a minute can seem like two hours. That's Relativity. Everything is relative."

我們往湖心出發。

「相對論其實很容易。」他直接就切入這個主題。

愛因斯坦不浪費時間，他盡可能不浪費任何時間。

「當你和一位漂亮的女孩坐在一起，對你而言，二個小時也不過像一分鐘那麼短而已，對吧？但是，當你坐在牙醫師的椅子上，牙齒被鑽來鑽去時，一分鐘的時間卻像是二個鐘頭那麼久。這就是相對論。每件事物都是相對的。」

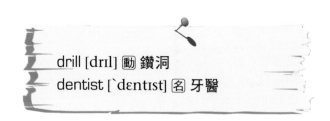

drill [drɪl] 動 鑽洞
dentist [`dɛntɪst] 名 牙醫

I knew exactly what he meant, but it couldn't be that easy. (It wasn't.)

As we headed across the lake, Einstein explained that before relativity, everyone had thought that the universe worked **according to** the laws of Isaac Newton.

我完全明白他的意思，不過不可能這麼簡單吧！（的確不是。）

　　我們穿越湖心的時候，愛因斯坦解釋說，在相對論提出以前，大家都認為宇宙是依據牛頓的定律運作的。

according to...　依據…

Isaac Newton was a scientist who lived in England about three hundred years ago. Newton saw the universe as a giant **clockwork** machine. You could **measure** any length, speed, or weight and get an exact answer that would not **vary** or change.

Everyone believed that, until Einstein came along and showed that the cosmos was actually a much stranger place.

牛頓是大約三百年前英格蘭的一位科學家。他把整個宇宙看做是一部巨大的鐘錶機器。人們可以測量各種的長度、速度或是重量，然後得到一個既不會更動也不會改變的準確答案。

　　每個人都相信牛頓的說法，直到愛因斯坦出現，指出宇宙其實不是我們所熟悉的那樣。

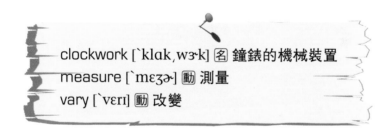

clockwork [ˋklɑkˏwɝk] 名 鐘錶的機械裝置
measure [ˋmɛʒɚ] 動 測量
vary [ˋvɛrɪ] 動 改變

Einstein realized that the length and **mass** of an object **depends on** how fast it is traveling. The faster the object goes, the more it weighs and the shorter it seems to become.

This is true for all things — racing cars, rockets, planets and whole **galaxies**. And at very *very* high speeds, even the passing of time itself can seem **altered**.

The only thing in the universe that never changes is the speed of light. It is always 300,000 km per second.

Relativity is a difficult idea because it means that how the universe looks depends on where you are looking at it from. Everything is relative to everything else. That was a lot to think about already.

"Hey! Watch out!" a voice shouted.

愛因斯坦瞭解到，一個物體的長度和質量與它運動的快慢有關。物體移動得愈快，質量愈大，而長度則愈短。

對所有的事物而言都是如此——賽車、火箭、行星以及整個銀河系。而且在非常非常高速的情況下，甚至時間本身的流逝也似乎是可以被改變的。

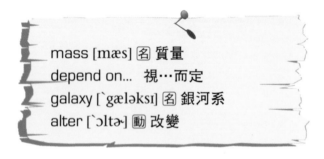

mass [mæs] 名 質量
depend on... 視…而定
galaxy [`gæləksɪ] 名 銀河系
alter [`ɔltɚ] 動 改變

宇宙中唯一絕不會改變的是光速，永遠都是每秒三十萬公里的速度。

　　相對論是相當難懂的概念，因為它意味著宇宙的樣子，決定在你觀看的角度。每一件事物都是與其他事物相對的。光是這個概念就已經有太多要思考的東西了。

　　「喂！小心！」有個聲音喊著。

I looked round and saw that a much bigger boat was on a **collision course** with us. Its engine buzzed loudly like a wasp ready to sting.

Einstein **adjusted** the sail and gave a friendly wave as we narrowly missed hitting them. He turned our boat gently toward the far shore then returned to science as if nothing had happened.

"Most of my relativity was based on thought **experiments** and a little **common sense**," said

Einstein. "But relativity is true for everything, from tiny **atoms** to massive stars and black holes in space."

"Cool," I said, brainlessly.

I already knew that Einstein had written the most famous **equation** in the history of science:'$E=mc^2$'.

From this formula, people realized that under the right conditions, a small **amount** of **matter** could be turned into a huge amount of energy.

我環顧四周，看見一艘比我們大得多的船正朝著我們駛來，就快要撞上了。它的引擎聲嗡嗡作響，就好像一隻隨時準備螫人的大黃蜂。

愛因斯坦調整了帆的方向，兩艘船差點兒就撞上了，他還對他們友善地揮了揮手。他將船緩緩地轉向遠方的岸邊，然後又回到原來的主題「科學」，彷彿什麼事也沒發生似的。

「我的相對論大多是基於思想上的實驗及一些常識。」愛因斯坦說。「但是相對論真的適用於每一件事物，從微小的原子到巨大的星體以及太空中的黑洞。」

「真酷！」我不加思索地說。

我早已經知道愛因斯坦寫下科學史上最有名的方程式：$E=mc^2$。

從這個公式，人們瞭解到在適當的情況下，一個質量極小的物質也可能轉變成巨大的能量。

collision [kə`lıʒən] 名 碰撞
course [kors] 名 航線
adjust [ə`dʒʌst] 動 調整
experiment [ık`spɛrəmənt] 名 實驗
common sense 常識，判斷力
atom [`ætəm] 名 原子
equation [ı`kweʒən] 名 方程式
amount [ə`maunt] 名 量
matter [`mætɚ] 名 物質

Other scientists worked on the idea and developed it further. It led to the atomic bombs which ended the Second World War with Japan.

"You must have been pretty proud of that," I said.

其他的科學家繼續研究這個概念並且加以發揚光大，結果造出原子彈，結束了對日本的第二次世界大戰。

「你一定對此相當引以為傲吧！」我說。

Einstein looked really sad.

"If I had known how my work would be used, I would have become a watchmaker instead of a scientist," he said, slowly shaking his head.

I didn't know what to say.

"That's enough for today," he **announced** suddenly, turning the boat around to **head for** home. "I'm tired."

"Of sailing?"

"Of thinking. I *never* get tired of sailing."

Our boat cut smoothly through the water and headed for the waiting shore.

愛因斯坦看起來相當難過。

「如果早知道我的研究工作會這樣被應用，我寧可成為一名鐘錶匠而不是科學家。」他緩緩地搖著頭說。

我不知道該說些什麼才好。

「今天就到此為止吧！」他突然冒出這麼一句話，同時將船轉向，準備回航。「我厭倦了。」

「厭倦了航行嗎？」

「是厭倦了思考。對航行我是從不會厭倦的。」

我們的船平穩地劃過水面，往等待我們的岸邊駛去。

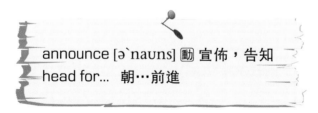

announce [ə`naʊns] 動 宣佈，告知
head for... 朝…前進

Trying not to puke

When I woke up on the morning of the Show and Tell I felt like **throwing up**. I hate speaking in front of people.

I got to school and found out that I was the last speaker before the lunch break. Great. I had all morning to **shuffle** my notes and think about being sick.

盡量別吐

「秀秀說說」這一天終於來了。那天早晨醒來時,我覺得想吐。我討厭在一群人面前說話。

我到學校後,發現自己竟是午休前最後一位上臺說話的人。這下子,我有一整個上午的時間把我的小抄揉來捏去,並且想著噁心不舒服的事了。

puke [pjuk] 勔 吐
throw up 嘔吐,反胃
shuffle [ˋʃʌfl] 勔 把⋯移來移去

The talk just before mine was Spider's. He sent everyone to sleep, **droning** on about the local bird life like they were his best friends or something.

Then, while Spider was still talking, there was a quiet **knock** on the classroom door.

在我之前上臺的恰好是史派特，他把大夥兒都催眠了，單調而沉悶地談論這兒的鳥類生態，彷彿牠們是他最好的朋友似的。

史派特仍不停地講，接著，一個沈穩的敲門聲在教室門口響起。

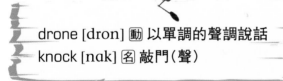

drone [dron] 動 以單調的聲調說話
knock [nɑk] 名 敲門（聲）

It creaked open and I saw Einstein's face appear in the gap. Our teacher, Mrs. Clark, nearly had **a heart attack** right **on the spot**.

Einstein slipped inside our classroom and sneaked into an empty desk on the third row.

He looked over his shoulder and gave me a big, **clumsy** thumbs up **sign**. He had made a real effort to look smart. He had even put socks on — one was red and the other was brown.

I've got to **admit** that having him there made me forget all about being **nervous**.

65

門嘎吱一聲開了，我看見門縫中露出了愛因斯坦的臉。我們的老師——克拉克老師差點兒當場心臟病發作。

　　愛因斯坦悄悄溜進我們的教室，鑽到第三排的一張空位坐下。

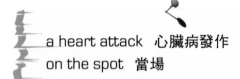

a heart attack　心臟病發作
on the spot　當場

他轉過頭，大大地對我比了個生硬的、拇指朝上的手勢。他下了好一番工夫讓自己看起來光鮮體面，他甚至穿了襪子呢！——一隻紅的，另一隻卻是棕色的。

我必須承認，有他在場，的確讓我全然忘了緊張這碼子事。

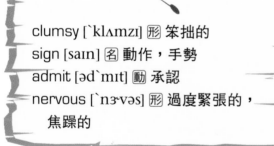

clumsy [`klʌmzɪ] 形 笨拙的
sign [saɪn] 名 動作，手勢
admit [əd`mɪt] 動 承認
nervous [`nɝvəs] 形 過度緊張的，
　　焦躁的

When it was my turn, I told them everything I knew about Einstein. It just came out like I'd always known it.

At the end, I explained how some other scientists had gone to Africa and Brazil in 1919 to study an **eclipse** of the sun.

Einstein had **predicted** that starlight would be seen to **bend** around the sun. It did and his theories were proven to be correct. It was after this that he became famous all over the **globe**.

輪到我的時候，我告訴他們我所知道有關愛因斯坦的每件事，一切都很順暢，就好像我一直都知道似的。

　　在結尾部分，我說明了在1919年時，科學家們去非洲和巴西研究日蝕的事。

　　愛因斯坦之前就曾預言，星光有可能會在太陽的周圍產生彎曲。事實的確是如此，他的理論也被證實正確無誤。就是在這件事之後，愛因斯坦享譽國際。

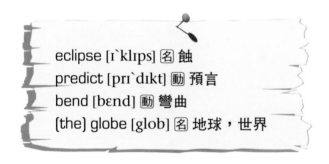

eclipse [ɪ`klɪps] 名 蝕
predict [prɪ`dɪkt] 動 預言
bend [bɛnd] 動 彎曲
[the] globe [glob] 名 地球，世界

Einstein sat there nodding every now and then and when I'd finished they all **clapped**. It was **brilliant**. Afterwards, Einstein shook hands with everyone — even Spider. He was a big hit.

He stayed around long enough to make sure I got an 'A' then we **sloped off** outside.

I had done it. It was the best feeling in the world.

愛因斯坦坐在那兒，不時點頭。當我講完時，大家鼓掌叫好。這真是太棒了！隨後，愛因斯坦和每個人握手——連史派特也不例外，愛因斯坦真是個了不起的大人物。

　　他待了好一陣子，確定我拿了個「A」之後，我們才溜到外頭去。

　　我終於做到了！——這真是世界上最美好的感覺。

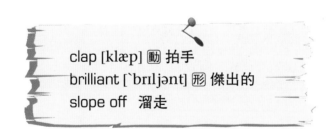

clap [klæp] 動 拍手
brilliant [`brɪljənt] 形 傑出的
slope off　溜走

71

New York City — today

That summer was the best time. I saw him **on and off** right until the end, a few years later.

Einstein died in 1955. I first heard about it on the radio and I was really sad. Dad bought all the newspapers the next day so I could keep the **clippings** about him. There were loads.

That was all a long time ago. But Einstein's theories and ideas changed the way we think about the universe for ever.

今日紐約

　　那年暑假真是美好極了。之後幾年，我還偶爾會看到他，直到他過世。

　　愛因斯坦在1955年過世。我先是在收音機裡聽到這個消息，我好難過。第二天，爸爸買了各家的報紙，好讓我可以保留有關他的剪報。我剪了好大一堆。

　　那已是好久以前的事了。但是愛因斯坦的理論和思想卻永遠改變了我們對宇宙的認知。

on and off　偶爾，斷斷續續
clipping [`klɪpɪŋ] 名　（從報刊等）剪下的東西

His was some of the most important and brilliant work ever done in science.

The name Albert Einstein is forever linked with the idea of genius: a man who can see further and clearer than those around him.

I know how smart he was, but when I think of Einstein, I don't think of the science and the formulas. I see him in his boat — adjusting a sail, or gently correcting the rudder. Always looking ahead for the next gust of wind that will send him speeding across the water.

他的研究是科學界中最重要且最輝煌的成果之一。

　　亞伯・愛因斯坦這個名字永遠和「天才」這個概念連結在一起：他就是這麼一個人，凡事都看得比他周遭的人更深入、更透澈。

　　我知道他是多麼地聰明，不過每當我想起愛因斯坦時，我想到的不是科學或公式，而是那個站在船上的他──在船上調整帆的方向或是輕緩地掌舵的他。他總是向前看，等待下一陣風揚起，帶他快速地穿過水面。

Timeline

Albert Einstein was born on 14 March 1879 in Ulm, on the River Danube in Germany.

1895 Expelled from school, aged 16.

1901 Begins work at the Federal Patent Office, while using his spare time to develop his work on Relativity.

1903 Marries Mileva Maric.

1905 Becomes a professor at the University of Zurich.

1905 Publishes his Special Theory of Relativity and three other scientific papers that change our understanding of the world for ever.

1915 Presents his General Theory of Relativity to the Prussian Academy of Sciences in Berlin.

1916 Einstein's General Theory of Relativity is published.

1919 Expeditions to Africa and Brazil observe an eclipse of the sun and prove that Einstein's theories are correct.

1920 Becomes famous across the entire globe.

1922 Wins the Nobel Prize for Physics.

1933 Flees Nazi Germany. Moves to Princeton in the USA and continues his scientific research.

1939 Writes to the American President to warn him that the Nazis are developing the atomic bomb.

Albert Einstein died on 18 April 1955 in Princeton, USA. He was 76 years old.

生平紀事

一八七九年三月十四日，亞伯‧愛因斯坦出生於德國多瑙河畔的烏爾姆。

1895　十六歲，被學校開除。

1901　開始在聯邦專利局工作，並利用空閒時間進行他在相對論方面的研究。

1903　與米勒華‧瑪瑞克結婚。

1905　於蘇黎世大學擔任教授。

1905　特殊相對論及另外三份科學研究報告出版，世人對世界的認知從此改觀。

1915　在柏林的普魯士科學研究院發表一般相對論。

1916　出版愛因斯坦一般相對論。

1919　英國皇家學會科學考察隊前往非洲和巴西觀測日蝕，證明愛因斯坦的理論正確無誤。

1920　成為聞名全球的人物。

1922　獲諾貝爾物理學獎。

1933　逃離納粹統治的德國，來到美國普林斯頓，繼續從事科學研究。

1939　寫信給美國總統羅斯福，提出納粹正研發原子彈的警告。

一九五五年四月十八日，亞伯‧愛因斯坦逝世於美國普林斯頓，享年七十六歲。

Glossary

atomic bomb 原子彈

a violent weapon which explodes with great power and can destroy life and buildings for huge areas around it

black hole 黑洞

an area in space which sucks matter and light down into it — nothing can escape from a black hole

cosmos [`kɑzməs] 名 宇宙

the universe

eclipse [ɪ`klɪps] 名 蝕

an eclipse of the sun is when the moon passes in front of it, blocking the sunlight

energy [`ɛnɚdʒɪ] 名 精力

when something is able to do work

equation [ɪ`kweʒən] 名 方程式

$e=mc^2$ is an equation. Each letter has a meaning, for example e is energy, m is mass and c is the speed of light. Equations can be used to work out the answers to difficult sums.

formula [`fɔrmjələ] 名 公式

a fact shown by numbers or letters

galaxy [`gæləksɪ] 名 銀河系

a huge group of many, many stars

physics [`fɪzɪks] 名 物理學

the type of science that studies energy and movement

mass [mæs] 名 質量

how much matter something contains

matter [`mætɚ] 名 物質

everything in the world is made of matter — it is something
which you can measure

relativity [ˌrɛlə`tɪvətɪ] 名 相對論

when something is compared with something else

theory [`θiərɪ] 名 理論

an idea

trajectory [trə`dʒɛktərɪ] 名 軌道

when something, such as a ball, is thrown, it can curve
upwards and then downwards — this curved path is its
trajectory

universe [`junə,vɝs] 名 宇宙

the planets, the sun, stars and everything

國家圖書館出版品預行編目資料

宇宙教授:愛因斯坦的故事=The cosmic professor:
the story of Albert Einstein / Andrew Donkin著;
Gillian Hunt繪; 錢怡君譯．－－初版二刷．－－臺北市:
三民, 2004
　　面;　　公分. (超級科學家系列)
　　ISBN 957－14－2992－9 (平裝)

1.英國語言－讀本

805.18　　　　　　　　　　　88003988

網路書店位址　http://www.sanmin.com.tw

© 宇宙教授:愛因斯坦的故事

著作人　Andrew Donkin
繪圖者　Gillian Hunt
譯　者　錢怡君
發行人　劉振強
著作財　三民書局股份有限公司
產權人　臺北市復興北路386號
發行所　三民書局股份有限公司
　　　　地址／臺北市復興北路386號
　　　　電話／(02)25006600
　　　　郵撥／0009998-5
印刷所　三民書局股份有限公司
門市部　復北店／臺北市復興北路386號
　　　　重南店／臺北市重慶南路一段61號
初版一刷　1999年8月
初版二刷　2004年1月
編　號　S 854890
定　價　新臺幣壹佰玖拾元整
行政院新聞局登記證局版臺業字第○二○○號

有著作權‧不准侵害

ISBN　957-14-2992-9　(平裝)

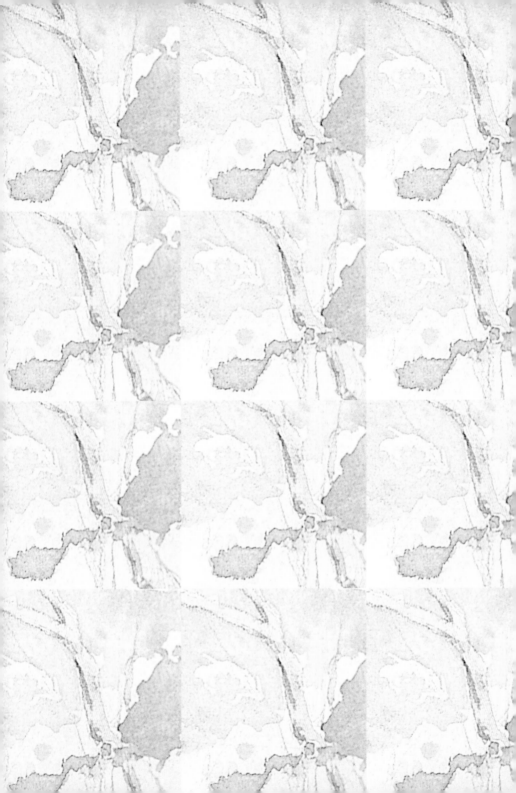